P9-EEC-984

Is it Time?

by Marilyn Janovitz

North-South Books

New York | London

Copyright © 1994 by Marilyn Janovitz
All rights reserved. No part of this book may be reproduced
or utilized in any form or by any means, electronic or mechanical,
including photocopying, recording, or any information storage
and retrieval system, without permission in writing from the publisher.

Published in the United States by North-South Books Inc., New York.

Published simultaneously in Great Britain, Canada, Australia, and
New Zealand in 1994 by North-South Books, an imprint of
Nord-Süd Verlag AG, Gossau Zürich, Switzerland.
First paperback edition published in 1996 by North-South Books.

Library of Congress Cataloging-in-Publication Data.
Janovitz, Marilyn.
Is it time? / by Marilyn Janovitz.
Summary: Rhyming questions and answers
lead a young wolf from bath into bed.
[1. Wolves—Fiction. 2. Baths—Fiction. 3. Bedtime—Fiction.
4. Sleep—Fiction. 5. Stories in rhyme.] I. Title
P28.3J263IS   1994
(E)-DC20   94-5100

A CIP record for this book is available
from The British Library.

The illustrations in this book were created
with colored pencil and watercolor.
Designed by Marc Cheshire

ISBN 1-55858-331-9 (trade binding)
1 3 5 7 9 TB 10 8 6 4 2
ISBN 1-55858-332-7 (library binding)
3 5 7 9 LB 10 8 6 4 2
ISBN 1-55858-545-1 (paperback)
1 3 5 7 9 PB 10 8 6 4 2
Printed in Belgium

Is it time to run the tub?

Yes, it's time to run the tub.

Is it time to rub-a-dub-dub?

Yes, it's time to rub-a-dub-dub.

Run the tub, rub-a-dub-dub.

Is it time to use the towel?

Yes, it's time to use the towel.

Is it time to give a howl?

Yes, it's time to give a howl.

Use the towel, give a howl,
Run the tub, rub-a-dub-dub.

Is it time to brush my fangs?

Yes, it's time to brush your fangs.

Is it time to comb my bangs?

Yes, it's time to comb your bangs.

Brush my fangs, comb my bangs,
Use the towel, give a howl,
Run the tub, rub-a-dub-dub.

Is it time to dress for bed?

Yes, it's time to dress for bed.

Is it time to tuck in Ted?

Yes, it's time to tuck in Ted.

Dress for bed, tuck in Ted,
Brush my fangs, comb my bangs,
Use the towel, give a howl,
Run the tub, rub-a-dub-dub.

Is it time to kiss good night?

Yes, it's time to kiss good night.

Is it time to switch the light?

Yes, it's time to switch the light.

Kiss good night, switch the light,
Dress for bed, tuck in Ted,
Brush my fangs, comb my bangs,
Use the towel, give a howl,
Run the tub, rub-a-dub-dub.

Is it time to go to sleep?

Yes, it's time to go to sleep.

Go to sleep and dream of sheep.